THE
CHILDREN *of* LIR

Sheila MacGill-Callahan

PICTURES BY
Gennady Spirin

Ragged Bears

For Patrick, Mary, Deborah, and Justin, four royal children S. M-C.

For my friend and teacher Michael Schwartzman G. S.

First published in 1993 in the United Kingdom by
Ragged Bears Ltd., Ragged Appleshaw,
Andover, Hampshire, SP11 9HX.

Originally published in the United States in 1993 by
Dial Books
A Division of Penguin Books USA Inc.
375 Hudson Street, New York, New York 10014

A CIP record of this book is available from the British Library
ISBN 1 85714 045 1

The art for this book was prepared with watercolors. It was then color-separated
and reproduced as red, yellow, blue, and black halftones.

Long ago there was a king in Ireland whose name was Lir. He had four children who were the light of his heart, each more beautiful than the other:

Twin boys with hair that flamed the red-gold of a summer sunset,

and twin girls with black hair shining like a secret pool at midnight. Only one thing marred the children's happiness. Their mother, Queen Aobh, had given her own life when the girls were born.

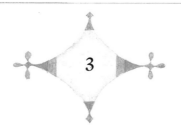

To ease their loneliness King Lir wed Aobh's sister whose name was Aiofe. Aiofe was fair to look at, but her beauty hid an evil heart. As time wore on and she bore no child, Aiofe grew jealous of her sister's children and plotted against them, for hers was the power of darkness.

When the king was away from home, she called the children to her. "Come," she said, "let us picnic in the woods and take our ease away from prying eyes, for today the day will be as long as the night, and light and darkness have equal claim upon the earth."

She led them into the forest where she spread a feast on white linen and bade them eat. No sooner had they raised the golden cups to their lips than they felt themselves change. No longer were they youths and maidens, but four swans who gazed at each other with wild fear and disbelief.

Aiofe's voice rose in a triumphant, gloating shout. "Swans you are and swans you shall remain for three times three hundred years, or until the Man from the North shall be joined to the Woman from the South."

The words fell on the hearts of Lir's children like stone, for they knew such a joining could never happen. The Man from the North and the Woman from the South were the names of twin mountain peaks that stood at the ocean boundaries of their father's kingdom. Unless the very earth should move, the peaks could never join.

Aiofe gave a satisfied nod. Then she continued,
"I grant that on this day every year when light and darkness are equal, you will regain human form and speech.
But on that day your feet may not touch the earth or
you will surely die."

She laughed, "I will give you one gift: You shall have
voices so lovely that you will be hunted as treasures for
the sweetness of your song."

The four swans took to the air, keening a wild lament.
Men in the fields ceased their plowing to gaze in wonder.
Women at the hearth or rocking the cradle felt their
hearts touched with a sorrow too great to be borne.

Word of the swans spread far and wide across the land and people came from all over Ireland to listen to their sweet music.

The country people built them a snug house on the shore of Inniskeel Island, provided with all they needed to live. They would sing on the warm summer nights, as men and women, nobles and peasants gathered to listen.

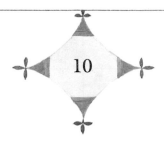

But Aiofe's jealousy and hatred burned stronger than ever, for the king could speak of nothing but his lost children.

In time his grief drove him mad, and he took to wandering far from the castle. Finally he came to the island of the swans and listened to their song, his face alight with happiness. Lir's children took loving care of him from that day forward, though he did not know them.

   With King Lir gone from the castle, Aiofe took
control of the kingdom and bided her time until the day
when dark and light would be equal. Then, she knew,
the swans would die.

   When the change back to human forms came upon
them, the four were flying far out over the sea, for
they too knew they must die and had chosen a clean
end beneath the waves. They sang together one final
song. Then down, down they fell into the sightless
depths, hand clasping hand, their hair streaming in a
red-black cloud.

   Suddenly they felt something solid beneath their
feet and were lifted above the waves as swiftly as they
had fallen.

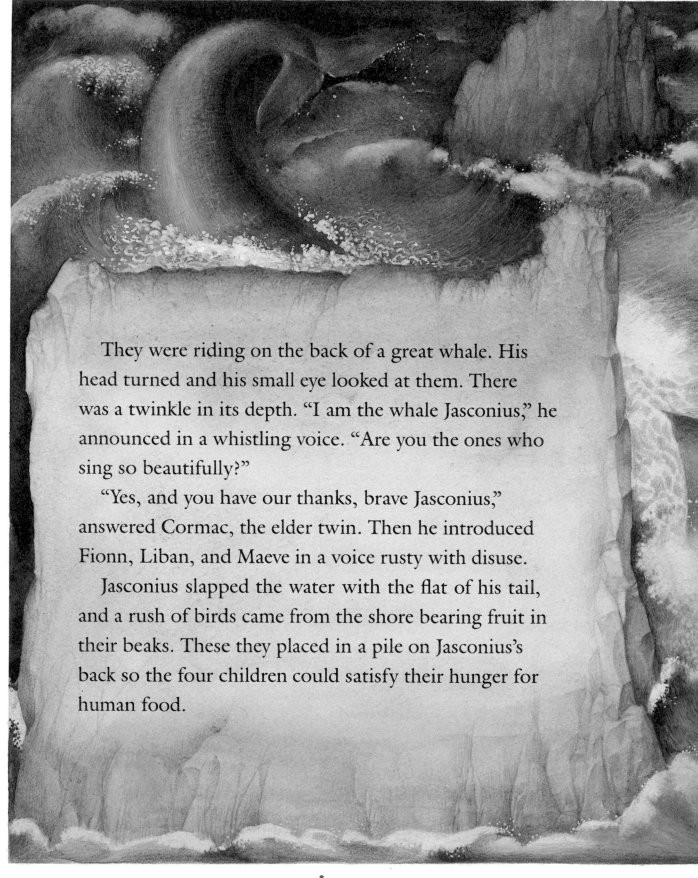

They were riding on the back of a great whale. His head turned and his small eye looked at them. There was a twinkle in its depth. "I am the whale Jasconius," he announced in a whistling voice. "Are you the ones who sing so beautifully?"

"Yes, and you have our thanks, brave Jasconius," answered Cormac, the elder twin. Then he introduced Fionn, Liban, and Maeve in a voice rusty with disuse.

Jasconius slapped the water with the flat of his tail, and a rush of birds came from the shore bearing fruit in their beaks. These they placed in a pile on Jasconius's back so the four children could satisfy their hunger for human food.

When they had eaten, the seals and dolphins gathered
in a circle in the water to hear their story, while the
birds perched wherever there was room on Jasconius's
broad back.

After the tale was told, Jasconius called for song.
The deep voices of the seals hummed in the background
while the dolphins and Jasconius whistled along with
the birds. The four royal children joined hands and
danced the night away in merry jigs and reels.

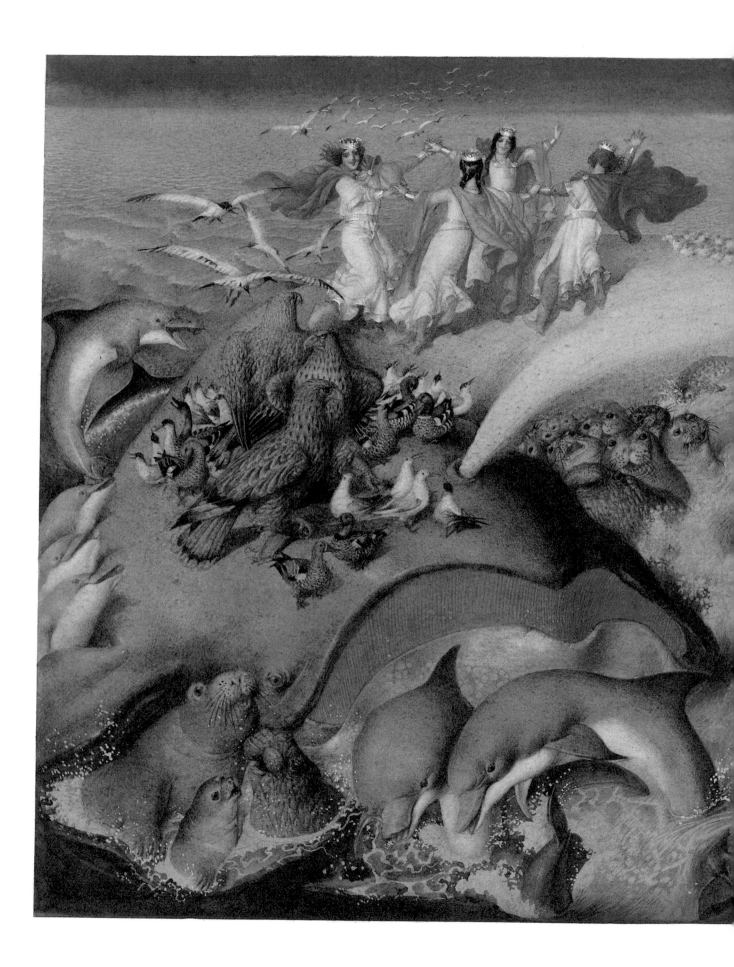

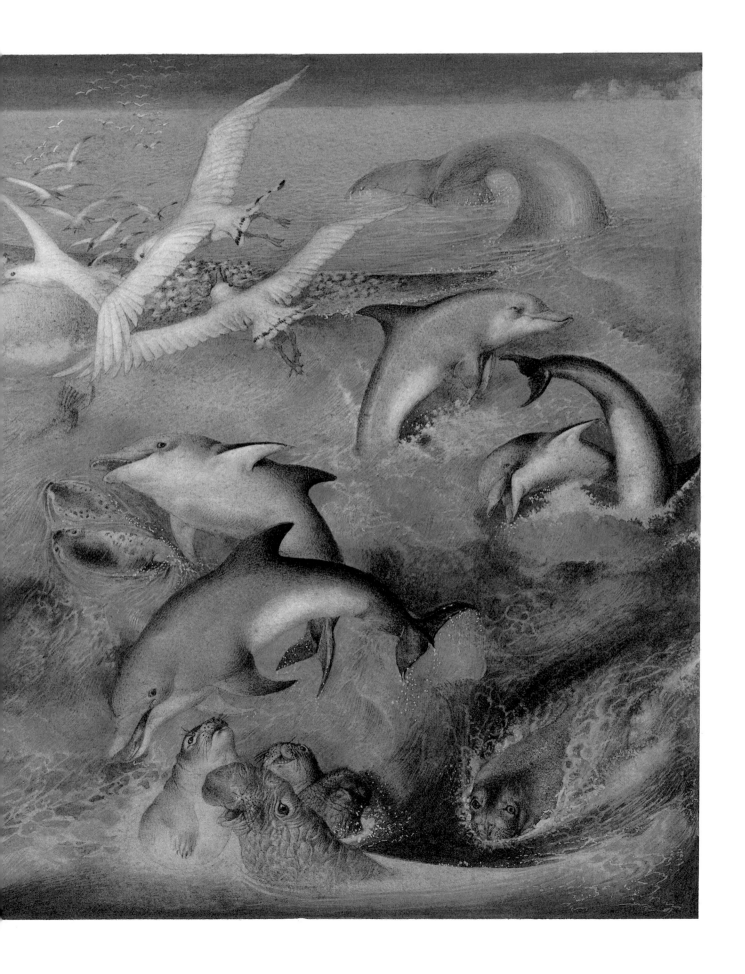

As the sun rose, they fell to rest. Liban wiped the sweat from her face as she said, "We have survived the first change. Now we must plan what may break Aiofe's curse before we turn into swans again."

They talked with Jasconius as the day wore on, but the riddle remained unsolved. How could the Woman from the South ever be joined to the Man from the North?

Just as the sun was about to sink, Jasconius spoke. "My heart is with you. I and all the other beasts will think long and hard but," his eye closed in a wink, "if you do not find your answer this year, do not fear. As surely as the sun now sets, I will always be there to catch you."

For seven years the riddle stood. Every year Jasconius was there to receive the swans. Now when their feathers fell away they were taller and older. And every year Aiofe's spies reported the return of the swans. In the seventh year she acted.

When the four returned from their visit to Jasconius, they found their home in ruins. King Lir did not come forth to greet them. Gulls, kestrels, larks, and wrens twittered around them in warning, but they paid no heed. So anxious were they for their father's safety that they did not see the men with nets waiting behind the tall stones.

All four swans were together when the weighted
mesh flashed out. They fought with their sharp beaks
and strong, webbed feet but to no avail. They were
carried back to the castle and the malice of the queen.

"I have you now, and I have your father who dared to
prefer you to me," she gloated. And for a year she held
them captive. Their only comfort came from the badgers
and the foxes who had secretly tunneled into the cave
where they were held. "Be of good cheer," whispered
a gray old badger as the day of change drew near. "We
have a plan." But then a guard came, and the badger
slipped away.

The day came. Aiofe declared a holiday for her followers. A feast was prepared on the beach at the foot of the twin mountains, the Man from the North and the Woman from the South. As the sun moved west, a cooking fire was lit and many made rude jests about roasted swan.

Maeve and Liban, Fionn and Cormac thought that nothing worse could happen. Then their father was led forth and made to sit where he would see the death of the swans he loved. He gave a great cry and covered his face with his hands.

Farther and farther to the west slipped the sun until it trembled on the brink of the western ocean. Queen Aiofe's face was wreathed in a gloating smile. "Sing, sing," she jeered, "for it will be the last time." Still, nothing happened. The heads of the four swans sank upon their breasts.

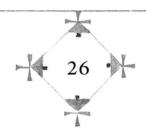

Then a huge spout of water arose in the bay as an enormous shape erupted from the depths. It was Jasconius! His tail slapped the water with a crack like thunder. On that signal a flight of eagles cut the air, grasped the net, and lifted it clear of the ground.

Still the change did not come. The sun seemed poised to see what would happen next. Aiofe urged her men to capture or kill the rising birds. They hurled spears and stones, but scored no hit. In the bay Jasconius was whistling shrilly and gazing at the twin peaks as if directing a dance. One by one the people on the beach turned, and their jaws dropped open in amazement. Between the peaks was a bridge of wild swans joined beak to tail, their wings beating as they held themselves in a proud arch. The sun slipped down as the last swan flew into place. The Man from the North was joined to the Woman from the South.

As Queen Aiofe shrieked and called her men to her, the eagles gently lowered the net. It now contained two warriors with red-gold hair and two tall princesses with hair as dark as a midnight pool.

Cormac stood forward, his sword red in the firelight. "Begone Aiofe! May the back of every hand be against you, may the fire refuse to burn for you, may the water refuse you refreshment, may wood and stone refuse to shelter you, and so may you come to the end of your days." He stood aside and Aiofe rushed forth, to be heard from no more.

The four embraced their father who shed tears of joy as the light of reason returned to his eyes. Jasconius became the kingdom's trusted counselor, and they had many a happy journey on his back during the warm summer nights.

King Lir's children lived long and happy lives, and they never lost the gift of song.

Some of the names of the people in this story are still used by Irish people. Here is the way they may have been pronounced long ago, and several still are today:

Lir · Lear	Cormac · *Cor*-mack	Fionn · Finn
Aobh · *Ay*-ve	Inniskeel · *Inn*-is-keel	Liban · *Ly*-van
Aiofe · *Ay*-fa or Ee-fe	Jasconius · Jas-*kone*-i-us	Maeve · May-vuh

◆

AUTHOR'S NOTE

The Children of Lir *is loosely based on an Irish myth. Lir is the Irish sea god, also called Llyr in the British and Welsh pantheons. Scholars believe that the Irish Lir is the far-off prototype upon which Shakespeare based King Lear, and the 12th century historian Geoffrey of Monmouth, his account of King Leir in* The History of the Kings of Britain.

Tradition places Lir's kingdom in the north of Ireland. There is a small island off the coast of Donegal called Inniskeel. Carved upon a stone slab are four swans and two men and two women. Each figure is in one of the angles of a cross twined with the Celtic symbol of eternity. Near the cross are four patches of green grass amid the stones.